D1486986

SO WHAT IF I'M A SORE LOSER?

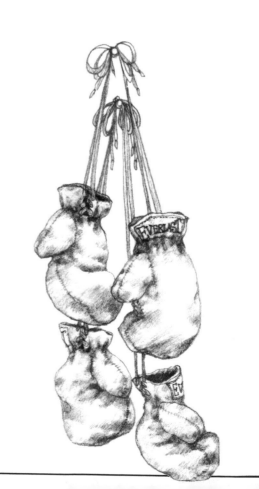

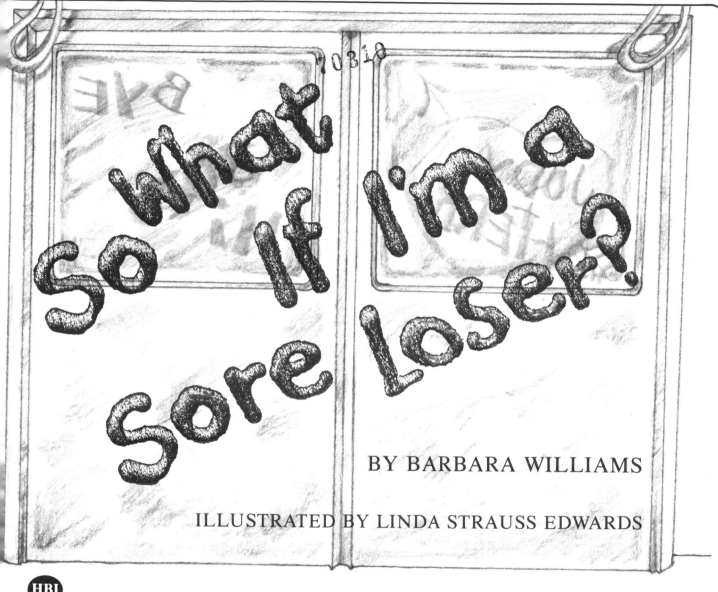

# So What If I'm a Sore Loser?

BY BARBARA WILLIAMS

ILLUSTRATED BY LINDA STRAUSS EDWARDS

HBJ

HARCOURT BRACE JOVANOVICH   NEW YORK AND LONDON

TO TAMMY AND TERESA

Requests for permission to make copies of any part of the work
should be mailed to: Permissions, Harcourt Brace Jovanovich, Inc.,
757 Third Avenue, New York, New York 10017.
Printed in the United States of America

LIBRARY OF CONGRESS CATALOGING IN PUBLICATION DATA
Williams, Barbara.
So what if I'm a sore loser?
SUMMARY: The constant competition between cousins
creates sore losers and equally sore winners.
[1. Cousins—Fiction.   2. Winning and losing—Fiction]
I. Edwards, Linda.   II. Title.
PZ7.W65587Sn        [E]        80-24783
ISBN 0-15-277260-X
First edition
B C D E

My cousin Maurice says, "Blake, you're a sore loser."
I say, "So what?"

Maurice lives across town in a big apartment house that looks out on the park.

I live right here in a small apartment house
that looks out on the small apartment house next door.

Maurice's apartment has a doorman who wears a coat with gold braid. He opens the door for you, whistles for a cab if you need one, and tips his hat.

Our apartment has a super who wears overalls and a dirty T-shirt. He opens the door for you, grumbles because you forgot your key, and scratches himself.

Maurice lives on the twenty-second floor
of his apartment and can choose
one of five elevators to ride up on.

I live on the fourth floor of our apartment
and always have to walk.

Mother says, "Stop complaining.
Climbing stairs gives you terrific muscles."

I say, "How come I still have un-terrific
muscles after climbing stairs all my life?"

Maurice has an aquarium with piranhas,
and two sets of boxing gloves,
and he knows how to play the drums.

Maurice plays the drums for his
piranhas because he says the rhythm
excites them.

His mother says, "For his age
Maurice is a very talented drummer.
Blake, would you like to hear
Maurice play the drums?"

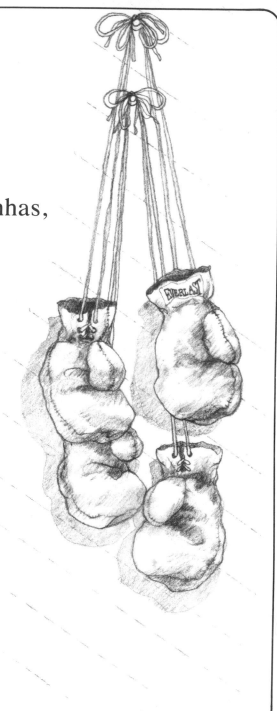

I have a window with pigeons outside, and a closet full of jigsaw puzzles, and I know how to hum.

I hum while I work my jigsaw puzzles because humming helps me think.

Mother says, ''Blake, if you can't at least hum a real tune, will you please knock it off before I go smack out of my skull?''

PIRANHA PUZZLE

SEVENTY TEENY WEENY PIECES

BOZO IN HAWA... JIGSAW FUN

CATERPILLAR P...

MAN of MARS

BIRDS OF PREY
JIGSAW

Maurice's apartment has a basement with a sauna and an exercise room and an Olympic-sized swimming pool.

Our apartment has a basement with a broken washing machine and some old clotheslines and Olympic-sized cockroaches.

Mother says, "It's nice Maurice can exercise in the basement of his apartment because he never walks up the stairs the way you do, Blake."

I say, "Maurice's muscles are too big already."

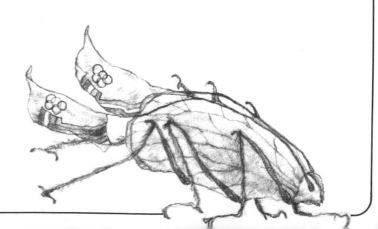

Maurice takes off his coat when it's snowing and eats all his broccoli and has a swimming teacher who says, ''Maurice, you'll be a champion swimmer in a few years.''

I keep my window shut in the winter and eat peanut brittle and have a dentist who says, ''Blake, you'll probably have to wear braces in a few years.''

Mother says, ''Blake, you're very lucky to have a cousin like Maurice who encourages you to eat vegetables and shows you how to swim.''

I say, ''Maurice's head is too big, too.''

Once a month on Sunday Mother and I take the subway across town to visit Maurice and his mother.

Mother and Aunt Connie throw their arms around each other and kiss and say, "Isn't it terrible that we don't see each other more often?"

Maurice and I shove our hands in our pockets
and squint at each other and think,
    *Isn't it terrible we have to*
    *see each other so often?*
    Aunt Connie says,
    "Maurice, be a polite host."

Maurice says, "Have some carrot juice."

I say, "No, thank you."

Maurice says, "Do you want to feed my piranhas? Ha ha ha."

I say, "You've played that joke on me already. Ha ha ha."

Maurice says, "Do you want to hear me play my drums?"

I say, "Not this year."

Mother says, "Blake, be a polite guest."

Aunt Connie says, "Maurice, why don't you take Blake swimming?"

I say, "I can't go swimming. I forgot my suit."

Mother says, "You can go swimming. I put your suit in my shopping bag."

I think, "How did she find my bathing suit in that jigsaw puzzle box?"

Maurice grabs his bathing suit and two towels
and both pairs of boxing gloves.

In the elevator he says, ''I can beat you
swimming and boxing. And I bet I can stay
in the sauna longer than you can.''
He flips me with a towel.

I say, ''Ouch, you're a bully.''

Maurice says, ''Shut up and be a polite guest.''

We put on our bathing suits,
and Maurice says, "Last one
in is a pair of smelly socks."
I'm a pair of smelly socks.

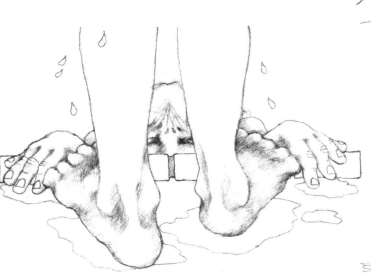

Maurice says, "Last one
to the end of the pool
is a pickled pumpkin."
I'm a pickled pumpkin.

Maurice says, "We'll swim
underwater, and the first
one up is a shabby skunk skin."
I'm a shabby skunk skin.

Maurice says, "*Oh boy oh boy oh boy oh boy! I beat you at everything!*"

I say, "You only won because you go swimming every day. Let's get out."

Maurice says, "Blake, you're a sore loser. I hate sore losers."

I say, "So what? I'd rather be a sore loser than a drowned loser."

We go into the sauna and stay there until our stomachs look like beets.

Maurice says, "The first one to leave is a pot of pig slops."

I'm a pot of pig slops.

Maurice says, *"Oh boy oh boy oh boy oh boy! I beat you again!"*

I say, "You only won because you practice going in the sauna every day."

Maurice says, "Blake, you're a sore loser. Sore losers make me sick. I hate sore losers."

I say, "So what? I'd rather be a sore loser than a boiled loser."

We go into the exercise room,
and Maurice hands me a pair of boxing gloves.
I say, "Only bullies punch other people."
Maurice clips me on the chin
and knocks me on my seat.
I say, "*Ouch,* you're a bully!"
Maurice says, "*Oh boy oh boy oh boy oh boy oh boy! I knocked you down!*"
I say, "You only knocked me down because you're a bully who punches people every day."
Maurice says, "I'd rather be a bully than a sore loser. You're a sore loser."
I say, "That's not where I'm sore."

One Sunday Mother says, "We can't go visit Connie and Maurice today because their apartment is being painted."

I say, "That's okay. I can manage."

Mother says, "So Connie and Maurice are coming to our apartment instead. Blake, I want you to treat Maurice just as nicely as he treats you."

I say, "I can't. I'm not strong enough."

Aunt Connie and Maurice knock on the door.
Mother says, "Blake, be a polite host."
I say, "Have some peanut brittle."
Maurice says, "No, thank you."
I say, "Do you want to stick your head
out my window and see what the pigeons
drop from the sky? Ha ha ha."

Maurice says, "Pigeons drop the same thing from the sky over our park. Ha ha ha."

I say, "Do you want to hear me hum?"

Mother says, "Not in this room he doesn't.

"Go to your bedroom and shut the door before you drive Connie and me smack out of our skulls."

I take Maurice to my room and say, "I bet I can put a jigsaw puzzle together faster than you can."

Maurice says, "You'll win because you practice every day. You know all of these puzzles by heart."

I say, "I'll choose this new Washington Monument puzzle that still has the cellophane on."

Maurice says, "You'll make me take a puzzle with more pieces."

I say, "This Washington Monument puzzle says 100 pieces on the box. You can choose a puzzle from that stack that says 79 pieces on the box."

Maurice says, "Okay, I choose this Grand Canal of Venice. I bet I beat you."

We spread out the puzzles and start to work. I hum just a little.

I say, "I'm finished! *Oh boy oh boy oh boy oh boy! I beat you!*"

Maurice says, "That's not fair. I think some of my pieces are missing."

I say, "*Ha ha ha ha ha!*"

Maurice says, "You're a sore winner. I hate sore winners! If there's anything in this world that's worse than a sore loser, it's a sore winner."

I say, ''I thought you'd never notice.''